TERRY DEA

KNIGHTS AND NIGHTMARES

Illustrated by Helen Flook

A & C BLACK
AN IMPRINT OF BLOOMSBURY
LONDON NEW DELHI NEW YORK SYDNEY

First published by
A & C Black, an imprint of Bloomsbury Publishing plc
50 Bedford Square
London WC1B 3DP

www.bloomsbury.com

ISBN 978-1-4729-0672-4

A CIP catalogue for this book is available from the British Library.

Printed and Bound by CPI Group (UK) Ltd, Croydon CR0 4YY

1 3 5 7 9 10 8 6 4 2

Terry Deary's Knights' Tales

The KNIGHT OF SILK AND STEEL

Illustrated by Helen Flook

A & C BLACK
AN IMPRINT OF BLOOMSBURY
LONDON   NEW DELHI   NEW YORK   SYDNEY

Chapter One
Sword
and Stew

A village in Germany, 1227

The dress was made of finest silk, but now it was faded and worn.

The dress was green with threads of gold, but the threads were broken and torn.

The dress reached down to the muddy road and the edge was tattered and splattered with mud.

The knight rode up to the tavern as the sun was setting and the sky was the colour of blood.

He handed his grey horse to the groom to feed and water it. The horse snorted softly as it smelled the oats and the hay.

The knight pulled his sword straight and walked to the door of the tavern. He pushed it open and looked into the gloomy room.

The room was a pit of filth from the straw on the floor to the ale that swam over the dirty wooden tables.

Some men supped from cups and others chewed on stew in wooden bowls. Some played board games and argued about their game – some just sat on their stools and argued because they wanted to argue.

Dogs wandered round and begged for scraps of stew but found the mutton too tough for their yellow teeth. (The sheep that was in the stew had died of old age.)

Leonard the landlord and his daughter Meg poured the ale from jugs and kept the fire and the candles burning, they slopped the stew and gathered up the empty plates and cups.

Meg was crop-haired, like a boy, and wore trousers when she worked in the tavern.

She saw the door swing open, letting in the dim, red light of dusk. She saw the knight. Her mouth fell open. She gave a scream.

The crowd fell silent. Fifty pairs of eyes were turned towards the door.

Meg tried to speak, but couldn't find her voice.

Sam the blacksmith had a voice and spluttered, "Mmmmf-mmmmf-mm-mm-mmmmf!" (His mouth was full of chewy stew, of course, but everyone in the tavern knew what he meant.)

"Just look at *him*!" Meg gasped at last.

John the gong-farmer sniggered.

Richard the rabbit-catcher giggled.
Simon the snaggle-bodger snorted.
Soon the whole room was
laughing and pointing, pointing and
laughing, slapping the tables, their
legs, their backs, rubbing their eyes
and rolling on their stools. (Helen
the harpist fell off her stool, but that
could have been the ale.)

At last the laughter died away.

"Good evening, ladies and gentlemen," the knight said in a voice as soft as fox fur.

"Ooooh! *Ladies*!" Tom the village fool mocked. "He's talking about *you*, Helen!"

Helen the harpist looked up from the floor.

"And gentlemen, he said. That's *you*, Tom Fool!"

The man at the door smiled gently. "I am Ulrich of Bavaria," he said, "and I am a knight."

"Yes, but what are you doing here?" Ben the badger-baiter cried.

"I am seeking a room for the night," said Ulrich.

"A knight's night sleep?" Tom Fool asked.

The crowd laughed.

"And a fight," Ulrich said, patting the huge steel sword that hung at his side.

The crowd went suddenly silent (except for Helen the harpist, who snored on the floor). Even the dogs went quiet and stopped chewing on the mutton that was tough as old leather.

No one wanted to fight with a madman.

At last the landlord's daughter, Meg, stepped forward. "We can offer you a room, sir, and some of our fine food!"

Sam the blacksmith, who was still chewing, said what he thought of the fine food. "Mmmmf-mmmmf-mm-mm-mmmmf!"

Ulrich bowed to Meg and thanked her.

"But, sir," said Meg. "I wonder if you could tell us all..."

"Yes?" said Ulrich.

"Why... Why are you wearing a green, silk dress and a long, blond wig?"

Chapter Two
Goats
and Greed

"It is a simple tale," Ulrich said, and he walked towards the bar of the tavern.

Leonard the landlord backed away. The shining steel of the swinging sword filled him with fear.

His daughter Meg was not afraid. "We love tales in this tavern," she said. "But we hear the same ones time and time again. If you have a new tale, then tell us, please!"

Ulrich leaned against the bar.

"I've travelled twenty leagues today.
I need a little food and wine to wash
the dust from out of my throat."

Leonard the landlord bowed so
low he almost scraped the floor.
"Of course, my lord, we serve the
very finest wine ... for those who
can afford to pay!"

The knight lifted a purse that
hung from the silken belt around his
dress. "I've money ... gold or silver,
groats or guilders,"
he said.

"A groat will buy you wine, and two will buy a plate of stew," Meg said merrily.

"That's *two* groats for our finest wine and *four* groats for our better stew," her father put in greedily.

Ulrich threw a piece of gold upon the counter top. "That should do to buy a drink for everyone here in the tavern... Keep the change," he shrugged, as Leonard the landlord snatched the coin. "When all my new friends have been served, then I shall tell my tale."

Ale splashed into cups, and from the cups slopped into mouths, while Ulrich drained the tavern's finest flagon of rich, red wine.

Meg made sure the man had only plates of lean beef stew and crusty white bread to mop the tasty gravy. The dogs looked up and dribbled down their chops to smell the meal that Meg had made.

At last, the tavern settled back onto their stools and looked towards the bar.

Ulrich was a handsome knight. He wiped his yellow beard carefully and looked around, and fifty pairs of eyes looked back. (Well, fifty-five, if we add in the dogs.)

"My name is Ulrich," he began. "My tale goes back to when I was a boy of twelve."

"I'm twelve," Meg said with a grin, and Ulrich nodded.

"I was a squire."

"I know what that is!" said Meg. "It's a boy who helps a knight – he fastens on his armour, cares for his horse and polishes his weapons."

Ulrich nodded once again, then went on with his tale. "My master was a lord of Alsace on the borders of France. Now, knights must have some deeds to do."

"Kill dragons!" Tom Fool said, but Ulrich shook his head.

"I've never seen a dragon, and I think they just exist in old stories told to frighten children. *Real* knights fight for what is right against the greatest evil of them all – wicked men!"

"Ahhhh!" the crowd inside the tavern sighed.

"But there is one fight greater than all other fights," the young knight said. "There is one thing that a knight may swear to live and die for..."

"I know!" Meg squealed. "Yes, I know just what you're going to say."

"A knight should find a lady fair that he can give his life to," Ulrich said.

"A lady *fair*!" Meg moaned. "My hair's as dark as coal."

Ulrich laughed. "When I say fair, I mean fair of face – or pretty.

She doesn't have to have fair hair!"
he said, and pointed to his own
blond wig.

"That's good," said the girl. "Carry
on. When you were twelve..."

"When I was twelve, I first met
with that old man ... Death."

The crowd let out a sorry moan.

Chapter Three
Wine
and Wig

"When I was twelve, my master fell in love with Isabel, the fairest lady in the whole of Austria."

"Then he married her," Sam the blacksmith groaned. "And they lived happy ever after. Pah! We've heard that tale a hundred times. We want the other tale – the one that tells us why you're wearing a green, silk dress!"

"Oh, silence, Sam!" came Helen's voice from somewhere underneath the table. "Let the knight tell us his tale in his own time."

"The Lady Isabel is married," Ulrich went on. "Her husband is a miserable man. He punishes his peasants, uses them as slaves, he's mean with money ... he lets fair Isabel dress in wool instead of silk.

"He holds no feasts and keeps no jesters, guests get dry bread, wine like vinegar and beds that have more fleas than fleece."

"We know his sort," said Ben the badger-baiter quietly. "Your master fought this wicked lord and killed him as dead as some duck's toenail?"

"Oh, no, my story has a much sadder ending," young Ulrich moaned, and sipped his rich, red wine. "My master went off to a joust – a mighty show of knights. Each knight takes it in turn to charge another knight with his lance. The knight who breaks the tip off his lance is the winner. He goes on to fight again and again till there is just one knight left ... the champion."

"Your master fought to be the champion and win his lady's heart?" Meg asked.

"He fought," young Ulrich sighed. "And lost?"

"And worse. A knight from France smashed his lance against my master's shield. The broken splints of lance went through the eyepiece of his helmet, through his eye and clean into his brain!"

"I bet that hurt," Richard the rabbit-catcher gasped.

Helen the harpist sat up straight. "Don't be a fool!" she cried. "It wouldn't hurt at all, for it would kill him dead!"

"It did," said Ulrich. "Such a mess." He supped his wine, as red as dead knight's blood. "I took his armour and vowed that I'd fight on. I'd win the lady's love, I'd fight a hundred knights – five hundred if I must."

"All very well," old John the gong-farmer said. "So you set off around the world to fight five hundred knights. There is a name for knights like that ... I can't remember what it is..."

"Knight errant is the name I think you want," Simon the snaggle-bodger smiled (so pleased to show how much he knew).

"Knight *errant* if you like," old John went on. "But still you have to tell us why you wear the dress!"

Ulrich nodded. "The Lady Isabel is married, so I cannot name her as my love. Instead, I fight for Venus, she's the mighty goddess of all love. I fight for Venus and, to make it plain, I *dress* as Venus! Venus wig and Venus dress," he said.

"And Venus beard?" Meg put in.

"No, I set off from Venice at least two years ago. And when you travel on the dusty roads it's hard to find a village with a barber who can give a shave. Some larger towns from time to time."

"Ah ha!" the crowd smiled. This was starting to make sense.

"So, here you are," the landlord said. "You'll stop the night?"

"I will."

"And then you'll travel on again."

The young knight spread his rein-stained hands and said, "I'd like a fight!" He drew his sword. The crowd stepped back. "Oh, not with you, my friends. I meant I want to find a knight to fight. The lord, perhaps, that owns this land?"

Chaper Four
Breakfast and
Butler

"Oooo-arrrrgh!" cried Simon the snaggle-bodger. "What you want's Lord Edmund up at Seckau Castle. He's your man, yes, he's your man."

"The Red Knight's what they call him," Helen the harpist laughed, then lay back on the floor.

"Red Knight, eh? Because he is a warrior, bold and mighty, dressed in armour scarlet red?"

"Nah!" sneered Tom Fool cruelly. "His old armour's red with rust."

Ulrich reached inside his dress and pulled out some parchment. "Here's a challenge to your lord. Take this to him. Tell him I'll meet him in the fields outside the castle after he has dined tomorrow noon."

"I'll take that!" Simon the snagglebodger said. He hurried through the door into the falling night. He whistled through the woods and haunting owls hooted back.

"I'm scared of bears!" poor Simon cried. "I must be mad to walk the woods on such a night."

But he soon saw the castle on the hill and flaming torches lit the gate. The guards were sleeping sloppily, the way they always did.

Simon simply walked right past and hurried up into the hall.

The lord of Seckau sat back, fat and full after his feast. "Ha! Simon! What do you want, lad?" he cried.

"A challenge, lord, from some young knight," the snaggle-bodger said, and waved the piece of parchment.

"Oh, I love a good fight!" Old Lord Seckau smiled and rubbed his hands with joy.

He called a skinny, white-haired servant dressed in black to stand beside his chair.

"Now, Charles, you'll need to work all night. I want my armour shining bright by morning, do you hear?"

"Huh, my lord, you don't want much. There's years of dust and rust to shift, and straps that snapped last time you fought. You do give me the rotten jobs!" the servant whined.

"I pay you well in wine and food and clothes and blankets for your bed, so stop your moaning, Charles. Do the job and wake me in the morning."

Charles raised his nose, and sniffed with hurt, but really it was all a game. By the time the cockerel crowed, the armour shone as bright as any silver moon.

His lordship had a little breakfast – seven eggs, and six beef pasties, five large wine cups, four sweet tartlets, three small cheeses, two roast chickens and a loaf of bread.

"Fetch my horse, my good man Charles!" he called.

The man in black raised his fine chin in the air and said, "May I remind you, I'm your butler, *not* your groom. That's the job for the stable lads."

Old Lord Seckau gave a mighty laugh and wrapped an iron hand around the shoulder of the servant. "Charles, my man, you *are* the groom!"

"Since when?"

"Since you *sacked* the stable lads and pocketed their wages. Now, help me fasten on the armour, then go down and saddle my charger. What I need is a little practice. After all, you wouldn't want your lord to lose!"

"Fah!" the servant spat. "I wouldn't mind."

"Oh, yes, you would," his master told him. "This knight Ulrich fights for trophies. If I win, I get a gold ring. If I lose, then *I* pay him. But see, my dear old servant... *If* I lose, then I will take the money from the wages that *you're* given to pay the grooms!"

"The what?"

"The money that you get to pay the grooms ... the money that you pay yourself, you black-hearted butler. So I lose nothing, you lose all!"

Charles went wobbly at the knees, then pulled himself up straight. "My dear, good Lord, of course you'll win! You always did ... when you were thin and fit and strong. I'll saddle your horse then come and help you climb aboard. The crane is ready in the castle yard!"

Chapter Five
Chargers
and Cheers

Dawn broke over the village tavern
and everyone was wide awake. The
tavern groom was brushing Ulrich's
fine, grey horse until it glowed
bright in the sun.

Leonard the landlord fed the
young knight fresh-baked bread and
honeyed ham, then Ulrich washed
in pure, clear water from the stream.

In the stable, young Meg took
the saddlebags and laid out all the
armour. "I can be your squire," she
told the knight. "Fasten up your
armour, lead your horse and pick
you up when you're knocked down!"

Ulrich nodded. "So you shall be. Venus would be pleased to see a girl who helps us fight her battle! Dust my armour while I put a stitch in this small tear I ripped in my dress!"

Meg was singing as she dusted. Ulrich was happy as he breathed in the morning's good, crisp air. "This is what a knight errant lives for. Fighting for his lady fair."

Ulrich pushed a wandering pig away then tucked his sewing kit into a saddlebag. With Meg's help, he strapped himself into his armour and slipped the dress on top.

The whole village gathered round and made a line along the road.

Ulrich clanged and clattered as he walked up the path to the hill. A line of cheery village people followed, work forgotten.

Charles had placed a row of
fences made from brushwood in a
line across the field. Old Lord
Seckau would ride down one side,
Ulrich's Venus down the other. When
they neared, they'd lower their lances
and each would try to smash the
lance tip on his rival's chest. If it was
a strong, true hit then one knight
could be smashed clean
from his saddle.

Ulrich mounted
on his charger,
and young Meg
passed up his
helmet. Seckau
waited at the
far end and
waved a cheery,
metal glove.

Charles the butler held a white rag.
"When I drop the flag, you ride.
God bless you! God bless us all!"

Each knight lowered the eye guard
on his helmet, each squire passed
his lord a lance. Fifty village people
held their breath and even birds fell
silent in the sky.

Charles the butler dropped the
flag.

Old Lord Seckau moved his heels and dug sharp spurs into his horse's side. The horse went *snicker*, gave a snort and moved at a gentle trot. (Well, it was old and his master weighed him down like castle stone.)

Ulrich spurred his fine, grey charger. The beast rose up on its hind legs and pawed the air like a dancing bear.

Then it lowered its head and struck the ground with hooves of thunder.

Off it sped towards Lord Seckau, faster than a speeding hare. Ulrich raced a hundred paces while Lord Seckau plodded ten.

The village cheered him, grass and clods of earth and worms flew up as he charged on while Lord Seckau plodded forth.

Lord Seckau brought his heavy lance down and took aim at Ulrich.

They were fifty paces apart.

Ulrich lowered his lance and tried to take aim at Lord Seckau, but it's hard to aim when you're galloping fast.

Forty paces, and Lord Seckau plodded almost to a stop.

Thirty paces, Ulrich's lance tip wobbled.

Twenty paces, Lord Seckau stopped and let his enemy race towards his waiting lance.

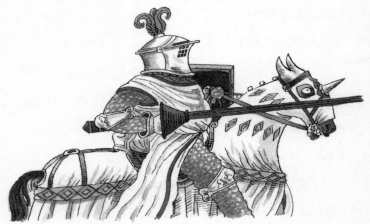

Ten paces, blond hair flew from underneath the helmet, green-gold silk dress billowed in the wind. Venus was a glorious sight riding for fair lady's love.

Three paces, Lord Seckau's lance tip crunched into the breastplate of

fair Venus. Ulrich's lance tip pointed
to the noonday sun. He'd missed ...
with worse shame to come.

Chapter Six
Lances and Legends

Old Lord Seckau sat there like a castle wall and did not move. As speeding Ulrich hurried past, the lance smashed him from his saddle. Ulrich tumbled backwards, skirt flying over his helmeted head.

Lord Seckau laughed.

Ulrich hit the green turf with a clatter that shook starlings from the trees a mile away.

Meg sobbed and ran across the grass towards the fallen man.

She pulled the helmet from his head
and threw the wig aside.

"My lord," she moaned.
"He's killed you dead!"

"I don't think so," Ulrich
whispered and gave a little gasp
for air. "Just help me to my feet,
my faithful squire."

The girl and Leonard the landlord dragged him up as Charles the butler helped Lord Seckau down.

The old lord grinned a red-faced grin and walked towards the unhurt Ulrich. "You young men are all the same," he said. "In too much haste. You need to learn that in a charge, swift deer don't beat a standing bull."

Ulrich smiled. "I'll learn, good lord." He reached into the leather purse that hung from his silken belt. "The payment for my lesson's one gold ring," he said, and passed the prize across.

The knights removed their iron gloves and shook each other's hand.

Someone caught the great, grey horse and led the way back down the hill.

Meg sighed. "You'll never win your lady fair if you don't fight more carefully."

Ulrich nodded. "Oh, I win as many as I lose. What matters is I play the game. I do my best and no one can do more. I'm not like all the other knights – the ones who stay at home and use their strength to beat and bully poor peasants."

They reached the tavern. Meg helped Ulrich take off his armour and pack it safely away.

"Can I come with you, Ulrich? Be your squire?" the crop-haired girl asked quietly.

The knight faced the sun that sparkled in the gold threads of his shabby dress.

"No, Meg, the greatest knights always ride alone. Go home," he smiled. "You'll have your own hard battles to fight, for life is often cruel." Then he climbed onto his horse and turned its head towards the west.

"I'll not forget you, or the lesson that I learned," Meg shouted after him. "I'll do my best and no one can do more."

The knight rode away from
the tavern as the sun was setting
and turned the sky to the colour
of blood.

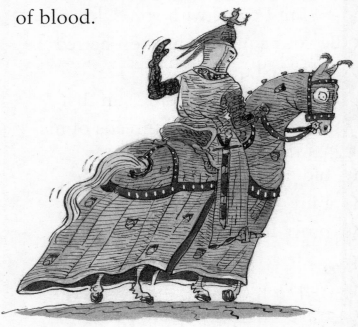

Epilogue

Ulrich of Liechtenstein was born in Austria in 1200. He fell in love with his master's lady (he says) when he was just twelve years old. He then travelled around Europe as a knight errant to prove his love by fighting anyone.

He set off on a journey from Venice to Vienna, and called his travels "The Venus Tour" because Venus is the goddess of love. He dressed in a long, blond wig and a woman's dress so he looked like Venus ... Venus with a beard. That was enough to put any enemy off!

Ulrich must have been very rich because he owned three castles and was able to offer a gold ring to anyone who could defeat him. Anyone who he beat had to give a gift to his lady and bow to the four corners of the Earth.

Ulrich said he broke 307 lances and won just as many fights. But he was not that great a warrior. He had to give away 271 rings, so he lost almost as many fights as he won.

We know about him because he wrote a long story-poem about his adventures and called his poem "Service of the Lady".

When Ulrich finished the Venus Tour, he rode to his lady's

castle. But what did she say? "Go off and do it again!" And when he had fought even more battles for her, did she fall in love with him? Sorry. No, she didn't. She was a hard lady to please.

The odd thing about knights was they liked to fight for a married woman ... a woman they could never win. Ulrich was disgusted with other knights of the time. He thought they were not true men. He wanted to show them how a real knight lived and fought ... even if he had to wear a dress to prove it.

Ulrich went on to be a great lord in Austria ... even with a broken heart. He died at the good old age of 78.

TERRY DEARY'S KNIGHTS' TALES

THE KNIGHT OF SPURS AND SPIRITS

Illustrated by Helen Flook

A & C BLACK
AN IMPRINT OF BLOOMSBURY
LONDON NEW DELHI NEW YORK SYDNEY

Chapter One
Drafts
and Deer

England, 1609

The castle is grim. The castle is grey. And the castle has a gruesome tale to tell.

The castle is known as Hylton Castle and it stands – grim, grey and gruesome – on a hillside by the River Wear in the north of England. You can see it there today – a sad shell of a hollow hall.

The castle is cold. The roof is gone, but the sun never shines inside the grim, grey, gruesome walls.

But when the last knight lived
there, the castle could be warm.
When the fire was lit in the Great
Hall, it was warm there by the fire.
Tapestry curtains hung on the walls
and kept out the draughts.

Chairs had cushions high and soft to keep out the draughts as you sat by the fire ... *if* you were one of the lucky ones that sat by the fire.

Lucky – like the last knight of Hylton, Sir Robert.

Logs as large as dogs flared in the fireplace and sparkled on the tapestry walls. Sir Robert took an iron poker and pushed it into the fire. Then he took a flagon of wine and emptied it into his silver cup.

When the poker was glowing red, he pushed the tip into his wine and watched it bubble and boil, spit and sizzle.

Sir Robert sat back in the chair and sipped the warm wine.

"Marvellous!" he smiled. It was a fat-faced, well-fed, red-cheeked smile.

Sir Robert stretched out a lazy hand and pulled on a rope that hung beside the fire. Somewhere in the castle halls, a bell jangled.

Moments later, the door opened and a girl hurried in. She was dressed in a fine, grey dress with a white, linen collar and an apron as white as snow.

Sir Robert, the last knight of Hylton, looked up. "Ah, Mary!"

"Yes, Sir Bobbert!" said the girl in a voice as dry as hay. Her throat went dry when she stood in the piggy-eyed gaze of her lord, and the words got jumbled in her mouth. "I mean ... Sir Robert, sir, sorry, sir."

"The weather, girl."

"Yes, sir," said Mary, and bent her knees in a low curtsey.

"Yes, sir *what*?" the knight rumbled.

"Yes, sir, whatever you say, Sir Bobbert ... Robbled ... Bobbit."

"I asked you about the weather. What's it like outside?" Sir Robert could have pushed open the shutters on the windows of the Great Hall, but he was too lazy for that.

"Sunny, sir," Mary panted, trying to remember.

"Sunny, eh? Marvellous!"

"And cloudy," she wittered.

"Uh? How can it be sunny if it's cloudy?"

"Sometimes it's sunny and sometimes it's cloudy. It changes. When a cloud crosses the sun, it stops being sunny and when..."

"Enough!" roared Sir Robert.

Mary trembled.

"Is ... it ... raining?" the last knight of Hylton asked slowly, as if he were talking to a slow and slightly stupid snail.

"Not today, Sir Bobble ... but it might rain next Tuesday, the wise woman of Wearside said in the market..."

"I ... do ... not ... want ... to ... know ... about next Tuesday!" he said. "If it is a fine day today, the deer will be out. Tell the Master of the Hunt I will go hunting this morning. Catch us a nice fat deer for dinner."

"Yes, sir," said Mary. She bobbed a curtsey and turned towards the door ... both at the same time. Her ankles became tangled, and she almost tripped over. "Ooopsy-daisy! Sorry, Sir Rubble!"

"And tell that useless stable boy ... Skeleton..."

"It's Skelton, sir. Roger Skelton."

"Whatever his name is ... tell Skeleton to have my bay mare ready, brushed and saddled."

"Yes, your lard-ship ... your lord-shap..."

"And take this wine away ... it tastes of burnt wood," said Sir Robert, passing the silver cup to the girl. "A quick nap and then I'll be ready to ride," he sighed. "Ma-a-a-a-rvelous!"

Chapter Two
Wine and
Warmth

Roger Skelton sat at the kitchen table. He supped at a bowl of broth that was hot from the pot that hung over the fire. His thin, round shoulders were covered in a thin, round jacket of green and his skinny hands trembled as he held the spoon. "I'm cold, so cold!" he murmured to himself.

The fire burned brightly and a whole pig hung on a spit over the flames. The spit had a wheel at one end, a wheel like the one on a watermill. Inside the wheel was a small, brown dog. The dog walked forward inside the wheel. As it walked, it turned the spit. As the spit turned, the pig turned over the fire.

The roast-pork smell filled the castle kitchens. The pig fat dripped into the fire and spluttered and spat and burned with a fierce flame.

The door crashed open and Mary the maid ran in.

"Oh, Roger, there you are. His lordship is going hunting in a while..."

"I'm cold!"

"He wants his best bay mare made ready," the girl went on.

"But I'm eating me dinner! I need it to warm me up. Didn't I tell you, I'm cold?" he whined. Roger was a whiner.

Mary placed the great goblet of wine in front of the boy.

"Sir Robert has just heated up this goblet of wine," she said. "Now it's wasted. Drink it and it may warm you up."

Roger wrapped his hands around the silver cup and felt them glow. "Ooooh! Warm."

"And it's warm *inside* if you sip it," Mary said. "Otherwise, I'll just have to throw it away."

Roger put the silver goblet to his lips and sipped. It was a mixture of fine wine and ash from the poker. It warmed his mouth, warmed his throat, then warmed his gut. The warmth began to spread over his body. "Ahhhh!" he sighed. "Lovely."

The warm spirit of the wine went up Roger's nose and made him a little dizzy. "Ooooh-eeeeh!" he said, and wobbled. A silly smile spread over his face and his eyes closed. Slowly, slo-wly, s-l-o-w-l-y, s-l-o-o-w-l-e-e-e-ee, his face fell forwards onto the table.

"Poor Roger," Mary sighed. "It's good to see you happy and warm for once, but I can't let you sleep." She rested a hand on his shoulder and jiggled it. "Wake up."

The boy opened his bright eyes. "Hello, Mary!" he said. "I must have dropped off."

"Sir Robert wants you to saddle his bay mare."

"Does he?"

"Yes, I told you. He's going hunting. You'd better hurry. You know how he hates to be kept waiting, especially when he's off murdering little deer."

Roger rose to his feet and wobbled a little. "Ooooh! That soup's made me all giddy," he giggled. "I'll go and saddle that grey mare now."

"*Bay* mare," Mary moaned. "Get it *right*, Roger, for goodness' sake."

"Bay ... grey ... play ... day ... way ... hay!" Roger grinned and wobbled towards the door. He pulled it open.

"No, Roger!" Mary cried.

Roger walked through the door and slammed it behind him. There was a crashing and a clattering, like a knight in armour falling off his horse and into a bucket of nails.

Mary tore open the door and said, "Oh, Roger, that's the pan cupboard!"

"Ooooh!" said the boy, and wobbled towards the other door.

"Wait!" Mary sighed. Roger stood as still as he could. Mary walked across to him and pulled the saucepan off his head. "Now, Roger, off you go and saddle Sir Robert's *bay* mare."

Roger dragged his feet into the stableyard. The feet didn't seem to want to go where he wanted them to go. He stepped into the stable and saw the pile of hay in the corner, ready to feed the horses.

"I'm cold," he said, as he sat in the hay and pulled some over him to keep warm. "Sir Robert likes a little rest after his breakfast." Then he lay back in the tickly bed.

Roger's eyes closed...

The horses snorted. Roger snored.
A sparrow twittered in the rafters.
Peace fell on the stables of Hylton
Castle ... for a little while.

Chapter Three
Whip and
Wrath

Sir Robert, the last knight of Hylton, woke from his nap. Hunting horns were blaring outside his window and that was what had roused him.

He opened the shutters and saw a grey sky as dull as the water in the castle pond.

"The girl said it was a sunny day," he growled. "I must remember to give her a thrashing when I get back."

He stamped across the room and bellowed like a bull for his servants. "My riding boots! Where are my riding boots?"

When a boot boy ran along the passage with the big, brown boots, the lord roared, "And I hope they're clean. One speck of mud and you'll be thrashed."

"Clean as a raindrop, Sir Robert," the boy said proudly.

"Marvellous!" the last knight of Hylton chuckled, as he pulled them on. "And my spurs – fetch me my best silver spurs!"

A groom of the chamber brought in the shining spurs, a heavy, green cloak and a riding hat with a pheasant feather stuck in the side. "Your riding clothes, sire," the man bowed and bobbed.

"Marvellous! Now I am ready to go!" said Sir Robert.

The groom of the chamber gave a slippery smile. "Haven't we forgotten something?" he asked in a teasing voice.

Sir Robert hated that. He hated it when servants were smart and smug. He kept his temper. "I *have* forgotten something ... I was just seeing if you remembered, George."

"Geoffrey."

"What?"

"My name is Geoffrey, sire!"

"Whatever your name is ... you have forgotten something," the knight said sharply.

The servant brought his right hand from behind his back. "I don't think so. Here it is!"

Sir Robert looked at the stick with the large, silver knob on the top. "My hunting whip. Ah ... yes ... of course!" he said, snatching it from the slippery servant's slimy hand. "You've passed the test, George. Well done!"

"Thank you, sire," the servant bowed.

"Marvellous! Now," the knight said, as he marched through the hall and threw open the front gate, "I'm ready to go. Lead on, huntsman!"

The huntsman stood by a pair of grey deerhounds. "I think you have forgotten something, sire," he said.

"I think not! I have my boots, my cape, my hat *and* my whip. What more do I need?" shouted Sir Robert. "What more? Eh? Tell me!"

The huntsman coughed into his hand. "Ahem ... your horse, sire, your horse!"

Sir Robert turned redder than a robin's chest. "Yes! Yes! I know *that*! I know. No need to tell me..." He looked around wildly. "I ... I told that Mary girl to tell the Skeleton boy to bring it round to the front door, didn't I?"

Mary the maid was standing at the kitchen door, just along from the main gate. She turned pale.

"Oh, no, Sir Blobber! You just said get it beddy ... I mean ret it geddy! I mean..."

Lord Hylton hated to look a fool. He strode toward the maid and raised his whip. "First ... *first* you tell me it's a sunny day..."

"It was when the sun set this morning ... I mean when the rose shine sunned this..."

"And then ... *then* you failed to tell Skeleton to fetch my horse!"

"Skelton, Roger Skelton, sir..."

"And now ... *now*!" he said, and raised the whip. "Now you call me a liar!"

The whip came down. Mary raised her hands to her head and turned away. The whip caught her across the shoulders and made her sob.

"I will go and ask Skeleton myself," the knight raged. "I will ask him if he was told to bring the horse to the main gate. I am a knight! I don't walk around getting my own horses, do I?" he asked and raised the whip again.

"Please, sir, no, sir!" Mary cried and scuttled back into the doorway.

The whip came down and missed her fleeing form. It hit the doorpost and made Sir Robert madder ... madder than a wasp with toothache.

"Someone will pay for this!" the knight screamed, and the ravens on the castle roof rose into the air in panic. "I'll kill Skeleton the skiver!" he roared.

Sir Robert Hylton marched off to the stables.

Chapter Four
Straw and
Sneezes

Roger Skelton was dreaming of eating a warm pie in a warm bed. As he was about to eat it, the pie was snatched from him by a skeleton...

"Skeleton!" came the loud voice.
Roger knew that voice. "Skeleton!"

Roger stirred in the hay and
slowly woke up.

Sir Robert Hylton was looking
over the stable door at his bay mare.
"Not saddled! Not even brushed!"
he shouted. Wait till I get my hands
on the boy ... Skeleton!"

Roger slipped deeper under the hay and tried not to breathe. But a sneaky seed of hay slipped up his nose. "Atch..." Roger almost choked as he tried not to sneeze. "Atch..." His nose tickled till his eyes wept. "Tchooooo!"

The hay blew away and Roger Skelton looked up at his master. "Good morning, Sir Robert," he said with a simple smile on his simple face. But it simply wasn't enough.

Sir Robert's face had been red with rage. When he saw the stable boy, it wasn't red any longer. It was purple as a ripe turnip. But his voice was soft. "My horse is not ready, Skeleton."

"Lame, Sir Robert. You can't ride her today. I was just coming to tell you."

The knight stood over the boy and let his riding whip swing loosely by his side. "What's wrong with the mare?"

"Loose shoe."

"Let me tell you what I am going to do, Skeleton. First I am going to beat you for lying to me. Then I am going to beat you for not having my horse ready. That sounds fair, doesn't it?"

"Yes, sir... No, sir!" Roger cried.

In the castle kitchens, the servants heard the screams and covered their ears to shut out the sound.

Then the knight did a stupid and evil thing. He turned the whip around so he was holding the tip, then he struck the stable boy with the large, silver knob on the handle.

Roger had just turned to see why his master had stopped, so he caught the blow on the side of his head. If there had been a light in his eyes, it went out like a candle in a storm. He fell to the floor. Lifeless.

Sir Robert panted. "That will teach you, Skeleton. Now don't think a beating means you've been let off your duties. I still want that horse saddled, eh, Skeleton?"

Roger Skelton would not be saddling any more horses.

Sir Robert lowered the whip and spoke in a quiet, friendly voice. "Come on, Skeleton ... you've taken the punishment, now let's forget about it and carry on, eh?"

Roger Skelton would not be carrying on any more.

The purple face of the knight turned pale. He grasped the boy's thin, green jacket and pulled him up. Roger hung limp as wet washing on a line.

"It's all right, boy, I forgive you," said Sir Robert. "Skeleton? You can't be dead ... no, you can't! I hardly touched you." The knight's face turned red again. "How *dare* you die

... you ... you ... miserable little worm! This sort of thing causes so much trouble!"

The knight dropped the whip in the straw and carried the stable boy to the door. No one was in sight. Sir Robert looked out at the horse pond. He picked up a couple of old horseshoes and slipped them into the pockets of the boy's green jacket. Then he carried the little body to the pond and threw it out into the deepest part.

The knight wiped his hands on his hunting jerkin, then marched back to the castle, silver spurs jangling on the cobbles, to where the huntsmen were waiting.

"Hunt's off today," he said. "Horse is lame – lost a shoe."

Mary the maid peered around the door. "Where's Roger, Sir Pobble?"

"Eh? Oh ... ran off ... thought I was going to punish him because the horse lost a shoe! Ha! Simple boy. I wouldn't touch him. No ... ran off. That's the last we'll see of him!"

But Sir Robert Hylton was wrong...

Chapter Five
Heaven
and Hell

Mary missed Roger. She went to the stables to see if he'd come home. She looked at the bay mare. All its shoes were nailed on tight. As she turned to go, a glint of silver caught the setting sun. Sir Robert's whip lay in the hay. She picked it up. The silver head was wet and red with blood.

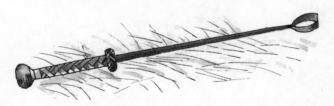

"Ohhhh, Roger!" Mary moaned. "What has he done with you?"

She searched the stable and barns and found nothing.

But two weeks later, Geoffrey the groom walked into the kitchen and sat at the table, shaking.

"What's wrong?" Mary asked.

"I was out walking Sir Robert's hounds today when I saw something floating in the horse pond. Some of the farm workers pulled it out. It was ... it was Roger's body."

Mary sobbed softly. "So that's what he did with him."

"Who?"

"Sir Robert," Mary said.

Geoffrey shook his head. "Lord Durham is here for dinner. Lord Durham is a judge for the county. There's going to be a trial in the Great Hall ... he says we can't have people thinking Sir Robert is to blame!"

"But he *is* to blame!" Mary cried. "The killer must be found and punished or Roger's spirit can never rest! Is the trial on now?"

Geoffrey nodded, and Mary raced along to the Great Hall. Sir Robert was sitting next to his friend, Lord Durham, and they ate slices of beef and bread from large plates in front of them.

Lord Durham munched and muttered, "How do you plead, Hylton?"

"Not guilty, my old fruit," Sir Robert replied.

"You didn't kill him, Bob?"

"Of course not, old bean."

Mary cried out in a clear voice, forgetting her fear. "He did! He said 'I'll kill Skeleton the skiver', and his lordship's whip handle was covered in blood."

Lord Durham glared at her angrily. "Silence in court!" He turned back to Sir Robert. "How did the blood get on the whip handle?"

The knight laughed and washed down his beef with a cup of ale. "Glad you asked me that. The lad, what's his name..."

"Skeleton?" Lord Durham said, looking at a scrap of paper.

"Skeleton," Sir Robert Hylton agreed. "He was asleep, so I gave him a little tap on the old noddle to wake him up. Must have had a thin skull, poor little chap. Died. Never felt a thing."

"They heard the screams down in the kitchens," Mary argued.

"Shut up," Lord Durham snapped.

"But..."

"Silence in court," the judge ordered.

"So how did Roger's body end up in the horse pond?" Mary said, bolder than she'd ever been.

Lord Durham turned to the knight. "I'm sure you can tell us that, Hylton, my friend?"

Sir Robert nodded his head sadly. "I tried to carry him to a doctor. But I slipped and dropped him ... just as I was passing the pond."

"Oh dear!" Lord Durham sighed. "I hope you didn't hurt yourself."

"No, but I got my boots a bit muddy trying to fish him out. In the end, I gave up. I mean ... he was only a servant, after all."

The judge spread some mustard on a piece of beef before cramming it into his mouth. "Yes, only a servant. But your story sounds good enough to me. I think ... pass me the ale, Rob, my old mate ... thanks ... I think I have to find you not guilty of killing him."

"Marvellous!" Sir Robert laughed.

Mary stormed to the table and slammed her fist down so hard that the silver plates and cups rattled. "You call that fair?"

Lord Durham and Sir Robert Hylton look at one another.

"Yes," they answered together.

Hot tears were pouring down Mary the maid's grubby cheeks. "Poor Roger will never rest in his grave. He'll haunt you, mark my words!"

Lord Durham pushed a plate of pork to one side so he could lean across the table and breathe his stinking breath in her face.

"Haunt us, will he?" he sneered, and spat crumbs on to the tabletop. "Push off, girl, or your master will haunt *you* with his whip."

That afternoon, Mary placed spring flowers on Roger Skelton's grave. "I hope you're warm now ... in Heaven!" she whispered.

But Roger *wasn't* warm and Roger *wasn't* resting in peace. His spirit, they say, returned to haunt the castle.

And, at night, when Sir Robert
Hylton tried to sleep – some spirit
seemed to haunt him. It was the
shadow of a boy in a green jacket,
hugging himself and moaning,
"I'm cold ... so cold!"

Long after Sir Robert Hylton had
gone to his own grey grave, the
spirit still wandered Hylton Castle.
And maybe it still does...

Epilogue

Hylton Castle is now in the city of Sunderland, north-east England. It was built around 1405, by William de Hylton, to guard the crossing point on the River Wear, about half a mile to the south.

Two hundred years later, the castle was owned by Sir Robert Hylton, a man with a fierce temper and a cruel streak.

Roger Skelton was Sir Robert's stable lad at Hylton Castle. His job was to look after the horses and keep the stables clean. But

Roger, they say, could be a little lazy. He really annoyed Sir Robert.

On 3 July, 1609, Sir Robert lost his temper with Roger Skelton one last time. He was furious when young Roger was too slow in bringing his horse. What happened next? There are a few stories:

• one says he speared the boy with a hayfork;

• another says he drew his sword and sliced off his head;

• another says he cut Roger's leg with a hay scythe and the boy bled to death;

• another says he beat Roger with his riding stick and cracked his skull.

But all the stories agree that Sir Robert threw the body into the castle pond. The body was found and it was clearly a case of murder.

Roger Skelton *may* have fallen on the pitchfork and *may* have cut himself with the scythe ... though he would not have cut off his own head (probably). It is pretty certain that he *didn't* throw himself into the pond.

Sir Robert Hylton was charged with the boy's murder. But he said it was an accident and, in September 1609, he was set free.

That much of the story is probably true. But then a legend grew up that said Roger Skelton came back and haunted Hylton

Castle. He wandered around crying, "I'm *cauld*!" (Now "cauld" is a northern word that can mean "headless" or "hooded" or simply "cold".)

One story says Roger Skelton was buried and his ghostly spirit rested. He was never heard of again. Another story says the Cauld Lad of Hylton never rested – his killer was not punished, so Roger is doomed to walk the Earth for ever more. Some people say they've seen him in the ruins of Hylton Castle to this day. Others say they've seen strange lights high up in the castle, even though the top floors have now crumbled and gone.

What do *you* think?

TERRY DEARY'S KNIGHTS' TALES

THE KNIGHT OF SWORDS AND SPOOKS

Illustrated by Helen Flook

A & C BLACK
AN IMPRINT OF BLOOMSBURY
LONDON   NEW DELHI   NEW YORK   SYDNEY

Chapter One
Boy and
Boar

England, 1485

Sir Thomas Stanley sat at the window and enjoyed the late-summer sun. It shone through the diamond panes of glass and on to his velvet jacket the colour of rust. He chewed on a peach and looked out over the fine garden of his castle.

There was a soft knock at the
door and Sir Thomas called,
"Enter!"

A boy pushed open the door –
a fair-haired, pale boy in a green
tunic. He was carrying a wooden
sword.

"Ah, George, my son! Come in,
come in!" Sir Thomas said, waving
a hand.

The boy stood in front of his father's chair. "You sent for me, Father?"

"I did, George, I did!" The man smiled. It was a wide smile and as honest as a snake that is just about to swallow a rabbit.

"I was practising my riding with a lance. Robin was teaching me."

"Good boy, good boy. We need all the knights we can get to fight our wars. There will always be wars and there will always be knights! Ha! Now, my dear, dear son..."

George blinked. His father had never called him 'dear' before. In fact, he thought his father hardly knew he was alive and living in the same castle. At dinner, his father sat with his favourite knights and ladies at the top table. George sat with the children and the squires.

"As you know," Sir Thomas was saying, "when a boy reaches your age, he is sent away to live with another family. It's a chance for a lad to see how other great families do things ... get to see other parts of England ... meet new people."

"Yes, Father."

"Now, I have the most thrilling news. It is so exciting I can hardly believe it myself, my dear, dear son."

"You are sending me away to serve as a squire to a knight."

"Not just *any* knight."

"A great knight?"

"Not just *any* great knight!" Sir Thomas Stanley chuckled. "You, my dear son, are going to serve in the palace of the king himself!"

"The king?" George said. "Why?"

"Why? Why what?"

"Why me? The king has thousands of fine families to choose from. Why me?"

Sir Thomas shifted in his seat as if it were hot. "Don't ask questions like that, boy. Now ... turn around and kneel before King Richard III!"

George turned slowly. Sitting in a darkened corner of the room, was a man with skin as pale as plaster. Dark eyes burned in a sad face with thin lips. The man was dressed in black. It was plain, black wool, not the fine silk George would expect from a king. Only a badge in the shape of a white boar on his riding cloak and a large golden ring on his finger gave some colour.

The king sat hunched in the chair and stared at George in a way that made the boy shiver.

A tall man was standing behind
the chair. He smiled a sneering
smile. George fell to one knee and
bowed before the king.

King Richard spoke in a harsh
voice. "Sir Richard Ratcliffe here
will be your keeper," he said.

The king stood up. He was not a tall man and he walked with a limp. He passed the kneeling boy and went to stand beside Sir Thomas. "He will do," he said.

Sir Thomas wrung his hands. "Oh, thank you, sire."

"Do not let me down, Thomas Stanley, or you know what will happen," he said quietly, and his voice was hard as frost.

Sir Thomas smiled a frightened smile and bowed low. Then the king was gone.

Ratcliffe slapped the boy on his back. "Get your servant – what's his name? Robin? Get him to pack your saddlebags. We ride for Nottingham Castle as soon as you are ready."

George hurried to the door.

"Goodbye, George," Sir Thomas said. There was something in the way he said it that made George think he meant 'Goodbye ... for ever'.

Chapter Two
Tudor and
Traitor

Robin groaned as he packed George Stanley's saddlebags. Then he spoke a curious rhyme:

"The Rat, the Cat, and Lovell the Dog,
Rule all England under the Hog."

"What does that mean?" George
asked.

Robin shook his head. He was
an old man, wise in the ways of
teaching a knight, but feeble in
body now. "I shouldn't have said
that! But ... but the Rat is the man
you've just met ... Sir Richard
Ratcliffe – one of King Richard's
most trusted knights. The Cat is
another ... Sir William Catesby.
And Lovell is Lord Francis Lovell ...
the king's favourite."

"They rule England?"

"With the help of the Hog – that's King Richard himself," Robin whispered.

"You can't call the king a hog!" George whispered back.

"It's his badge – a wild boar – a hog," Robin explained.

"Robin?"

"Yes, Master George."

"Why are we whispering?"

"Ah ... the man who made up that rhyme about the Rat, the Cat, and Lovell the Dog, was called Collingham. When the king heard about it, he had Collingham executed. So never call Ratcliffe the Rat!"

The old servant gripped the boy by the shoulders. "You are heading into terrible danger, Master George."

George shook his head.

"I'm going to train to be a knight. I may be knocked off my horse once or twice, but it's not real danger!" he smiled.

Robin did not return the smile. "Is that what your father told you?" he asked.

"Yes," George said. "Why? Would father lie to me? What is the truth?"

The door to George's room was open and Ratcliffe stood there with his sour mouth turned down at the corners. "Truth about what?"

George had learned Robin's lessons well – a knight does not show fear. "What is the truth about my journey to Nottingham?"

Ratcliffe glared at the boy. "England is in terrible danger," he said, and he sat on a stool by the door. He took out his dagger and used the point to clean his nails as he talked.

"*Danger?*" George asked.

"There is an enemy of the king called Henry Tudor – he has landed in Wales and he is gathering an army. He wants to take the throne from King Richard."

The boy gasped. "And the king wants *me* to fight?"

Ratcliffe sneered. "No, the king wants your *father* to fight. Your father and your uncle Will can command five or six thousand men. The king needs those men in his army. There is a great battle coming.

One of the greatest England has ever seen. King Richard has to win it."

"He'll win with my father's help," George said. He had seen the soldiers in the fields outside the castle, and watched them train, with the archers sending so many arrows into the sky that the sun turned dark.

Knights practised their fighting on horseback and on foot – swinging swords and axes and heavy clubs they called maces. They rode back into the castle each night to rest and seemed happy. The Stanley army was ready to fight.

Sir Richard Ratcliffe stood up and placed the knife point under the boy's chin. "Yes, young George. With your father's help we *will* win ... but what if your father does *not* help?"

"Not help?"

"What if your father turned traitor and fought for Henry Tudor? Then we would lose. You see the problem?"

"Why would my father fight for Henry Tudor?"

Ratcliffe nodded. "I suppose they don't tell you things like that. Henry Tudor is your father's stepson … *your* stepbrother. Sir Thomas may switch sides and fight for Henry. So, we need a *hostage*." The knife tip pricked the soft skin of George's throat. "And if your father betrays King Richard … then you know what will happen?"

Suddenly George *did* know. "You will kill me?"

This time, Ratcliffe gave a real, wide smile. "Oh, yes, little George. We will kill you!"

Chapter Three
Cheers
and Chains

The ride to Nottingham was grim.
George was always watched by three
men-at-arms. His servant Robin was
forced to ride at the back with the
baggage wagon and Sir Richard
Ratcliffe hardly spoke.

Nottingham Castle loomed above them and even on that summer day it seemed cold and unfriendly.

The fields outside the town were littered with tents of all sorts. Some fine ones with coloured stripes for the lords and some ragged shelters for the poorest archers and foot soldiers.

Cooking fires covered the fields with a haze of smoke, but through the smoke George could still smell the foul scent of the toilet pits and the filthy men.

From time to time, he saw knights practising with lances, while soldiers watched and cheered from the banks.

The gates in the city walls were crammed with people hurrying in and out, carts carrying food and weapons, beggars trying to cadge coppers and teams of huge horses pulling mighty bronze cannon along the roads.

Ratcliffe's small troop waited for the traffic at the gate to clear, and that allowed Robin to catch up with George on his pony.

"Look at the crowds!" Robin said cheerfully. "If you slip away, they'll never find you in this mob!"

"Slip away?"

"Escape! Save your life, Master George. The first chance we get, we'll flee. My family in Lancashire will look after you till this is over ... even if Henry Tudor wins, your father will be safe."

"So I will be safe?"

"No, no!" Robin moaned. "If your father helps Henry Tudor to win, then you will be too dead to enjoy the victory – Ratcliffe will see to that!"

The men-at-arms pushed George ahead and through a gap in the crowd. Inside the city walls, the market stalls were in danger of being crushed by the masses and even the houses were shaking. Only the mighty castle looked safe and solid. But, once he was inside, George knew he would never escape.

As they came near the gatehouse, he looked around. His guards were talking to the soldiers at the gate. Robin sat at the back of the line and nodded his head. The old man

climbed down from his pony, stiff
and aching from the ride.

George took one last look and
tumbled down from his saddle;
as soon as his boots touched the
cobbles, he was running back
down the road.

Robin swept a cloak over the boy's
head and dragged him down an
alley and into a doorway.

They were lost before Ratcliffe
knew they were gone. The doorway
led into a tavern. The tavern was
jammed with men looking for ale to
wash away the dust of the scorching
day. There was no way to fight their
way through the crowd.

Robin saw a gap between two women and slipped into it, but the gap closed before George could follow. He was stuck at the doorway.

There were angry voices in the alley and a young woman cried, "They went that way, my lord ... into the tavern..." then, "Ohhh! Thank you, sire," as Sir Richard Ratcliffe handed her a piece of silver from his purse.

Soon Ratcliffe's sunburned face loomed over George and his strong hand grasped the boy's hood and dragged him from the doorway.

"I should kill you for this, you little puppy. And when the battle is over I *will* kill you. No matter what happens, I *will* kill you!" he snarled. "For now, I need you alive ... but your old servant will die in the castle dungeons as soon as we find him."

Robin, however, was nowhere to be seen.

"A knight – a true knight – would not try to escape from a promise his father made. From now on," Ratcliffe said, "you will not be treated like a young knight. You will be treated like the miserable prisoner you are. From now on, you will be held in chains – chains as hard as King Richard's heart."

Chapter Four
Tower and
Torment

The army marched from Nottingham
two days later. It stretched for miles
along the English roads.

At its head was the round-shouldered shape of King Richard III. And, just behind him, his prisoner, chained to a pony and guarded by the menacing Ratcliffe.

The king led his army westwards to where he knew the enemy were coming. "You will see how a knight fights," Richard promised the boy. "What is your name, young Stanley?"

"George, Your Majesty."

"Ha! George, eh? I had a brother called George, you know?"

"No, sire."

"Yes, *brother* George," he said bitterly.

"What happened to him?" the boy asked.

"He betrayed us. Took sides with our enemies ... I had to have him executed in the Tower of London. My own brother. You cannot trust anyone. And I do not trust your father."

"He's still my father," George said. "I cannot call him a traitor."

King Richard nodded. "You are a good knight – and a loyal son. I had a son, you know."

"I didn't know."

"He died. A baby. Children die. You shall die if you father betrays me. Are you afraid?"

"No, sire."

Richard laughed and rode on.

That night, they reached a field that the soldiers called Bosworth. They set up their camp in the warm, evening air.

To the south and the west, the hills were gentle and green. In the distance, the sky was clouded orange.

Ratcliffe looked out of the tent where George was chained to the main pole. "Only an army makes a dust cloud like that. Henry Tudor is on his way. Tomorrow there'll be a battle."

"What will happen? George asked.

"We will win," the tall knight answered. "You see, we are on a hilltop. Henry Tudor's men will have to march *up* the hill to attack. We will mow them down with our arrows, and they will be climbing over the corpses of their friends. If any of them *do* reach us, they will be too exhausted to fight our knights. We sit here. We wait. We win." The man raised an arm and pointed to the north. "See that hill a mile away?"

"Yes, my lord."

"That's a place called Coton. Your father and your uncle are marching their army there now. When Henry Tudor attacks us, your Stanley armies will smash them from the side. We cannot lose."

George nodded. He lay back on
a blanket. After a long day's ride
he soon fell asleep. Deeply asleep.
Yet he awoke in terror.

Hours had passed. It was darkest
night. He wondered what had
woken him. Then he heard it again.
The screams of a man – a man in
torment. He knew it came from the
next tent.

Sir Richard Ratcliffe stumbled in
the dark of their tent and threw on a
cloak. He came back moments later

with his arm around a shadowy figure. "It was a dream, just a dream," he murmured to the man.

The shadow-man gave a long groan. "It's a sign, Ratcliffe, a sign. A bad sign. Tomorrow ... tomorrow in the battle ... tomorrow, I will die!"

And the boy knew the tormented voice was the voice of King Richard.

Chapter Five
Night
and Noon

King Richard sat on the floor of
the tent and took deep breaths as
if he were in pain. "Oh, Ratcliffe,
the things I saw!"

"It was a dream, Your Majesty."

"Maybe, Ratcliffe ... or maybe the gates of Hell opened up. The devil let out the spirits of the men and children I've murdered."

"You don't believe in spooks, Your Majesty," Ratcliffe said in a soothing voice.

"Remember Lord Hastings? He was my loyal friend. One night at dinner, I had him dragged outside and said I wouldn't eat till his head was cut off. The guards found a plank of wood and used that instead of a block. A sword instead of an axe. I saw him last night, Ratcliffe! He came back to haunt me!"

"Hush, Your Majesty. The men
will take it as a bad sign. They will
be afraid before they go into battle."
But the king wasn't listening.

"The Princes ... my
nephews ... my
brother's boys.
Locked in
the Tower.
Smothered
to death and
buried in a
secret grave."

"No, they were sickly children.
They would have died anyway,"
Ratcliffe argued quietly.

"They died without a funeral –
that means their spirits can't rest. I
saw them, too, last night, Ratcliffe."

"A dream, Your Majesty."

"Ghosts, Ratcliffe. And I saw Lord Rivers ... and ... ohhhh! My brother George! Did I tell you about George?"

"The traitor?"

"He asked us not to behead him. He said if we *had* to execute him, we should drown him in a barrel of wine!" the king sobbed. "Poor George. I saw him, too – he came to my tent. It is a sign, Ratcliffe, a sign." The king moaned again and sank back on to the ground. In the darkness, young George heard him breathing heavily. The boy fell into a restless sleep, too.

The noise of the camp, stirring at first light, woke him. King Richard sat up and looked across in his direction. The king's face was as grey as any ghost. He turned to Ratcliffe. "The boy?" he said. "The boy heard what I said last night."

Ratcliffe gave a single nod.

The king rose to his feet. "We can't have him telling the world that Richard is a coward – spooked by dreams like a child," he hissed. "If the battle goes against us, he *has* to die. Make sure it is done."

The two men turned towards the boy, their faces as twisted and ugly as ancient trees.

George looked back steadily.

A hooded man set George free from his chains. The battle had been thundering in the valley below, and George had been forgotten.

The hooded man also wore a mask that covered his face. He opened the lock and led George to the door of the tent. They looked down into the valley.

"What's happening?" George
asked, anxiously.

The man spoke in a voice muffled
by the mask. "Richard's first line
charged down the hill at Henry
Tudor," the guard said, and pointed
to the valley to the west.

"Lord Ratcliffe said they'd wait
here!" George argued. "He said it
would be a mistake to charge off
the hilltop!"

"A mistake," the man nodded. "It was. But it seemed the king didn't care to be careful. It seemed as if he was ready to die. He rode down at the head of the second charge... See? There he is!"

George could make out the round-shouldered knight in fine armour leading a charge of knights in the noonday sun.

They rippled like a silver stream in the light. But the army at the bottom were ready for them – a green flag with a red dragon waved over Henry Tudor.

The king's knights struggled to reach it, to smash the invader. But the dragon's soldiers chopped them down and swallowed them up.

On Coton Hill another army,
the Stanley army, sat and watched.
As the king's men died, Sir Thomas
Stanley did nothing to help. George
would die for that treachery, he knew.

At last, King Richard's horse was
brought down and soldiers with
axes and swords swarmed around
him like maggots over a piece of
meat.

Chapter Six
Helmet
and Hood

"To the rescue!" Sir Richard
Ratcliffe cried, as he gathered a
fresh troop of knights. It was too
late to rescue the king. All they
could do was rescue his body.

A great cheer from the valley
showed the Tudor army was
winning.

Sir Richard Ratcliffe rode up to
where George and the guard stood.
As he turned to make his charge
down the hill, he looked back.

"Execute him!" he shouted at the man in the mask. "Kill the traitor's son!"

George gave a tiny smile. Of course – the man in the mask wasn't just an *ordinary* guard. He was an *executioner* – men only wore masks if they had to execute their victim.

Ratcliffe slammed down the face-guard on his helmet. He lowered his lance and rode down the hill to join his king.

George turned to the man in the mask, who carried no axe, no weapon of any sort.

"My father *knew* I'd die," the boy said, "yet he did nothing to help."

The executioner shrugged. "Your father said he has other sons. If you die, he will not be broken-hearted."

George nodded. "Thank you, Father!" he shouted across the valley to the army that sat under the

Stanley banner of yellow and green. The army that didn't lift a finger to save its king.

"Your father will be all right," the masked man said. "Henry Tudor is his stepson. The Stanley family will be rewarded well for what they did today."

"And my reward? The axe? Or the sword? Or will you smother me like the princes in the Tower? Or drown me in a barrel of wine like the other George? You have no weapon. How will you kill me?"

The executioner raised a withered hand to the top of his head ... and pushed back the hood. Then he grasped the leather mask and tugged at it. "You have no idea how hot it's been inside this hood," he groaned.

He gave a last pull and threw the
mask away.

George stepped back and leaned
against the tent pole.

The executioner grinned at him.
"You don't really want me to kill
you, do you?"

George looked at the old man –
Robin, his servant. "No, Robin,
I think I'd rather live."

The old servant wrapped the boy in a tight hug and the two laughed till they had no breath left.

The king's defeated soldiers were struggling back up the hill, running past the boy and his servant. Away from the terror of the Tudor invaders.

Robin turned north and led George towards the Stanley army and his father. A treacherous army. A silent army. Silent as the grave.

Epilogue

King Richard III came to the throne of England in 1483. Some say he had murdered his nephews, aged around ten, to make sure he got the throne. They were taken as prisoners to the Tower of London and never seen again. Richard had no pity for children.

Richard had only been on the throne for two years when his kingdom was invaded by Henry Tudor. Richard made his last stand at Bosworth Field.

Still, with the help of Lord Stanley he *should* have crushed the invader and saved his throne. Just to make sure Stanley fought well, Richard held Stanley's son, George, as a hostage. If Stanley betrayed him, then the son would die.

The night before the battle, Richard suffered terrible nightmares – maybe haunted by the thoughts of the people he had killed.

At the last battle, Richard charged down the hill with his knights – the last great charge of armoured knights in British history, maybe even the world. Stanley betrayed Richard, and King Richard III died fighting as a knight. There would be no more battles like that. The world

of the knight was over for ever.
Even the bravest knight was no
use against the cannon that
armies had started to use.

Henry Tudor, the winner, took
the throne and became King
Henry VII. He was the first of
the ruthless Tudor kings and
queens of England. If Henry
had lost the Battle of Bosworth
Field, we would never have had
his son, the famous Henry VIII,
or granddaughter, Elizabeth I,
as rulers of England. All of
England's history changed on
that one day, 22 August, 1485.

Sir Thomas Stanley, the traitor,
was safe when his stepson Henry
won the battle. But the Rat, the
Cat, and Lovell the Dog were not.

Sir Richard Ratcliffe died in the battle. Lovell's skeleton was found in a dungeon a year later – it seems he had starved to death.

It was fine and glorious to be a knight ... but only when you were on the winning side.

George Stanley, the hostage, *should* have been killed by Richard's men when his father refused to fight for the king. For some reason, George was allowed to live. We don't know why – this story gives a possible reason, but it is only a guess. The truth is, it's a history mystery.

TERRY DEARY'S KNIGHTS' TALES

THE KNIGHT OF STICKS AND STRAW

Illustrated by Helen Flook

A & C BLACK
AN IMPRINT OF BLOOMSBURY
LONDON NEW DELHI NEW YORK SYDNEY

Chapter One
Bullies
and Berbers

Castile, Spain, 1099

Cristina hated the feasts at the palace of Valencia.

The knights made a lot of noise and shouted at her. But that wasn't why she hated the feasts.

The cooks in the kitchen made her run and fetch heavy bags of corn, pots big enough for her to bathe in and logs that were larger than her. But that wasn't why she hated the feasts.

The maids poked fun at her tattered, woollen clothes and her bare feet, for she only had shoes for church on Sunday. They bullied her. But that wasn't why she hated the feasts.

The feasts went on deep into the night. By the time Cristina had helped clear the tables, clean the pots and polish the pans, it was dark.

Even in the warm, summer nights, when the stars were like a shower of silver, it was dark in the streets of Valencia when she hurried home. *That* was why she hated the feasts.

Everyone was asleep as Cristina ran home over the stony streets, past snarling dogs, slippery rats and green-eyed cats. And worse.

That first night, she almost lost her way from the palace gates to her home on the hill below. She crashed through the door into the poor, little house and the leather hinges almost snapped.

Cristina's mother gasped in the blackness. "Who's there?"

Cristina panted for breath and creaked like the door. "Mama!"

"Cristina? Are you back?"

"Mama!"

"What on earth is wrong, child?"

"I saw a giant... He tried to catch me, but I ran. And when I ran, all the dogs started to chase me. He had huge arms and he tried to catch me. Oh, Mama! Do I have to go back to the palace?" she sobbed and threw herself on her mother's blanket.

Mama held her trembling young daughter and said, "We are at war, my child. The Berber enemies are at the gates of the city. Your father is in the army. We are alone."

"I know, Mama."

"I can't make enough money to keep you, Cristina. You have to help. You're big enough now. And when you work at the palace, you are fed for free."

"I know... It's not the work ...
or the girls who are so cruel to me.
It's... It's the *dark*. I hate the dark.
Giants get you in the dark."

Mama took her daughter by the
hand and pulled her to her feet in
the soft darkness of the room. She
led her to the door and pulled it
open. She looked down the street.
"See? No giants."

"On the corner, two streets down from the church," the girl breathed.

"Let's go and look at this giant, shall we?"

"No!" Cristina squeaked.

"Yes, I would like to see him. I was always taught that giants were just monsters from old tales. I would like to meet one."

The woman took her daughter firmly by the hand and led her out into the starlit streets. She pulled the girl up the hill, back towards the palace, past the church.

"Where is the giant?" Mama asked.

Cristina raised a thin finger and pointed towards the groaning, rustling shape ahead of them.

The woman nodded.

"As I thought. It is Master Sancho's windmill. The city needs his flour, so he works all night to feed us."

"No giant arms?" the girl asked.

"Just windmill sails," her mother said. "But if they scare you so much, then on the next feast night, come back across the fields."

"Yes, Mama ... wait for me, Mama!"
Cristina cried and ran home.

But on the next night, the girl
again ran from the palace and
almost fell into the house in her
fearful, fainting state.

"I saw a Berber... He tried to
catch me, but I ran. I almost ran
into him in the dark. I bumped into
him and he smelled terrible. It must
be a Berber... They've broken into
the city."

Mama took her daughter by the hand and pulled her to the door. "Let's take a look at this Berber."

And in the fields, the sour-smelling monster stood, flapping in the wind and grinning at the cloudy sky.

Mama shook her head.

"A scarecrow, Cristina. It's just a scarecrow. You are a *babieca*."

"What's that, Mama?"

"An idiot, Cristina. I'm sorry, but you are an *idiot*."

Chapter Two
Ham
and Horse

Cristina slept badly, with dreams of scarecrows that snatched at her hair and spun her round like the sails of a windmill.

The sun rose into another blue sky and another hot day lay ahead.

Cristina would sweat over the cooking fires in the castle kitchens and taste no cool air till the evening. She plodded wearily up the hill, looking at the dusty road and keeping her bare feet away from

sharp stones. Suddenly, there was a
monstrous crashing of iron on stone
as a troop of knights rode down
from the castle.

Every huge warhorse was led by a
young man in a tunic of his master's
colours. Pictures of swords and
dragons, crowns and leopards in

reds and golds, blues and silvers, purples and greens and whites.

Their armour glittered, and flags on the tips of their lances made a rainbow of colour.

Cristina was dazzled, and stood gaping while the hooves made sun-bright sparks on the paved street.

An old man dragged her into a doorway. "Don't step in front of that lot, foolish girl!" he said.

"Where are they going?" she asked.

"To attack the Berbers, of course," he laughed. "Those Berbers have been sitting outside our walls for months while we get short of food and water. Now El Cid will lead out his knights and slaughter them all.

There will be blood and Berber
bodies to mop up tonight! Hee!
Hee!"

"Who is El Cid?" Cristina asked.

The old man pointed to the
warrior who rode on the white
horse at the front. "That man there."

Cristina studied the face of the leading knight. "That's Lord Rodrigo," she argued. "I've served him at feasts."

The old man sighed. "Lord Rodrigo Díaz is King Alfonso's greatest warrior ... so the people call him El Cid – The Champion."

"I see. And will he beat the Berbers?" Cristina asked.

"The Berbers know all about him," the old man said. "When I was a soldier, I learned that battles are not won by the best fighters – they are won by the bravest. A scared army is a beaten army."

"And the Berbers are scared of El Cid?"

The man nodded, his eyes glinting in the light of the gleaming armour.

"Oh, yes. Their soldiers will tremble, their swords will shake and their arrows will rattle in their bows. Their teeth will chatter and their legs will be ready to run like rabbits."

"Just by *looking* at El Cid?"
Cristina smiled. "But I served him
roast ham and cabbage last night.
He is such a gentle man."

"He is a lion in battle. And he
is riding a lion, Babieca."

The dust from the hooves filled
the warm air and choked Cristina.
"Don't call me that. My mother
calls me that. It isn't nice."

"Eh?" the man asked, and
scratched his thin, grey beard.
"I didn't call you anything."

"You called me *babieca* – idiot," said Cristina.

"I said that El Cid is *riding* a lion, *Babieca*. His *horse* is called Babieca."

"Is it?" Cristina blinked and rubbed dust from her eyes. The last of the horses had passed. Trumpets sounded and a great cheer rose from the army on the city walls as El Cid and his knights rode out.

The old man hobbled up the hill towards the palace, and Cristina fell into step with him.

"Babieca is El Cid's warhorse," the man explained. "The Champion's godfather was a monk. His gift to young Rodrigo was his pick of any horse from the stable.

"El Cid picked a horse that his godfather thought was weak and useless. The monk cried 'Babieca!'.

Rodrigo laughed and said 'That's a good name for him!' and so the horse is known as Babieca. Of course, it has proved the greatest warhorse in all of Spain."

"Even an idiot can be a hero," Cristina sighed. "I wish I could be a hero ... but I'm such a coward. I'm scared of scarecrows in the dark."

The old man smiled. "We are all heroes. You never know how brave you are until you are tested. Trust me, girl – one day you will find you have a heart as big as Babieca."

Chapter Three
Boar
and Blood

The palace kitchen was busier than ever that day. And it was full of excitement.

Lord Rodrigo's wife, Jimena, came into the kitchens with orders for roast swans and whole boar with apple sauce. Tonight there would be a great party for the knights' victory.

"Have they won, then?" Cristina asked a cook, Ramon.

"Not yet," the red-faced, sweating man spat. "But we will, of course. El Cid is the master of terror. The enemy never know what he will do next. That is why Rodrigo is known as The Champion. The Champion of Terror!"

The palace servants worked all day, and by sunset the tables were piled with the richest food Valencia had. The poor people in the city may be starving, but the knights would eat like gods.

Yet when the doors to the grand hall opened, it was a quiet and miserable troop of dusty knights that wandered in.

"Did we lose?" Cristina asked.

Ramon scowled. "I don't know," he said. "But our lord Rodrigo is not with his knights."

The girl was about to ask more when Lady Jimena burst through the kitchen door and spoke to Ramon in an excited voice. "I want food for my lord Rodrigo."

The cook bowed low and began to say, "The feast is ready in the grand hall, as you ordered—"

But she cut him off. "To my lord's room. Broth. A simple broth with a little bread and warm milk."

"Is he unwell?" Ramon gasped.

Lady Jimena turned on him, furious. "It is not for *you* to ask questions. Just do as you're told."

Ramon shrank and bowed again. "I will bring the broth..."

"No, I don't want you in there. Send this girl," she said, pointing to Cristina.

"As you wish, my lady," the cook cringed.

Jimena was gone and Ramon hurried to obey. He found a small tray for Cristina to carry and led the way to the servants' stairs. "Up here and it's the large double doors ahead of you."

The girl took the tray and made her way up the dim stairway to the top. It led to a corridor and finally

to the doors, which were guarded
by a weary knight.

The knight stopped her, picked
up the spoon and tasted the soup.

"It's not poisoned," Cristina said.
"We would never do that."

The knight opened the door and
let her into the bedroom. Jimena sat
at one side of a great bed that had
curtains pulled back. The shutters

were closed and the room was gloomy. A doctor was standing over a man, who lay on the bed. "Put the food down on this table," the doctor said. "He may eat something later."

Cristina did as she was told and backed towards the door.

"Here, girl, hold this bandage tight while I cut it," snapped the doctor.

Cristina came near the bed and saw Lord Rodrigo lying there. A bandage was wrapped around his throat. As she watched, the cream linen cloth began to turn red with blood.

"Can't you stop the bleeding?" Lady Jimena moaned. "It's only an arrow ... just an unlucky, stray arrow."

"But it has gone deep into the neck – just where his helmet joins with his breastplate," the doctor said.

Lord Rodrigo, El Cid, gave a gurgling moan. Frothy blood trickled from his mouth and he half choked on it while the doctor looked on, helpless. The lord gave one last cry and went still.

The doctor lifted the knight's wrist. He shook his head and looked across the bed at Lady Jimena. "I'm sorry, my lady. Your lord is dead. El Cid is no more."

Lady Jimena looked at the doctor and then at Cristina. "Then we are all dead. All dead," she said.

Chapter Four
Candle
and a Coward

"I'm not dead!" Cristina whispered.

Lady Jimena reached across and stroked the girl's dark hair. "No, my child, no. But today the Berbers saw Lord Rodrigo fall. They chased our knights back into Castile. We only just closed the gates in time."

"But the walls will keep them out!" Cristina argued.

The doctor sighed and spoke slowly. "The Berbers will sit there and stop food getting into the city.

When hunger and disease have made us weak, they will attack and swarm over the walls. They will show no mercy. They may spare the life of a poor girl like you, but they will make you their slave."

Lady Jimena shook her head. "I think they will not wait. The plains are burning with the summer sun. I think they will want to finish us off quickly. I think they will attack tomorrow."

The three sat around the body of their lost leader.

"The Berbers are brave, but Lord Rodrigo terrified them," the doctor sighed. "Just the sight of him made them turn and run."

"I'm the same with windmills ... and I'm even afraid of scarecrows," Cristina said. "The other night I ran home crying because a man of sticks and straw frightened me. I am a coward."

"No, you're not," Lady Jimena said softly. "You didn't run away from a man of sticks and straw! You ran away from a man in the dark. You didn't know he was just a scarecrow."

Cristina nodded. "If I'd known it wasn't a real man, I wouldn't have run," she agreed.

Lady Jimena frowned. "If the Berbers know Lord Rodrigo is dead, they won't run," she said slowly. "But if they thought he was still *alive*..."

"They wouldn't attack tomorrow," the doctor said.

"But he *is* dead," Cristina said. "Dead as a scarecrow."

Lady Jimena turned her wide, brown eyes on the girl. They shone in the light of the single candle by the bed. "But no one *knows*. Only you, and Doctor Alvarez, and me."

"You mean ... we tell everyone that Lord Rodrigo is *alive*?" Cristina asked.

"That won't work!" the doctor moaned. "The Berbers won't believe it ... unless they see him."

"So, let them see him!" Cristina cried, for she suddenly knew what Lady Jimena was thinking. "Show them a scarecrow!"

The doctor almost laughed. "Dress our dead master in his armour? Put rods and straw inside to keep him upright? But how do we march him onto the battlefield?"

"Let him ride!" Cristina said. "Let Babieca carry him into battle." This time the doctor did laugh. "It would never work. Babieca is a warhorse. He needs someone to ride him ... or lead him. We can't just put

a corpse on his back and expect
him to lead the troops on to the
field of battle."

"Get a squire to lead him,"
Cristina said. "All the knights have
young men to help them!"

"No!" Lady Jimena
said sharply. "The
city is full of spies.
No one, *no one*
must know that my
husband is dead.
We cannot trust a
squire, or even a
servant – there are
even some knights
who hate my husband. No. *We* must
prepare the body. *We* must mount
him on Babieca. One of *us* must lead
him into battle."

The doctor shook his head, uncertain. "My lady, my legs are too old to walk through the town and through the gates and onto the fields outside the city."

"And I cannot do it ... everyone knows me. It would look odd. The Berbers would know it was some sort of trick."

Lady Jimena and Doctor Alvarez looked at Cristina.

"Me?" the girl gasped.

Some words echoed in her head. She remembered them from that morning. *We are all heroes. You never know how brave you are until you are tested.*

The time had come for Cristina the coward to be tested.

"I'll do it," she said. "If you will help me, I'll do it."

Chapter Five
Wood
and War

Cristina's first task was to run down to the kitchen to fetch wood and straw. When she reached the kitchen door, she took a deep breath to calm herself.

"What are you doing, girl?" the cook Ramon asked. "You were meant to take broth to El Cid, not take bowls to the Berber army, too. Where have you been?" Before she could answer, he went on, "Not that you are needed. The knights aren't

hungry tonight. They are too
miserable about El Cid's wound."

"He'll live to fight another day,"
said Cristina.

Ramon smiled a wide smile. "Did
you hear that, everyone? Our lord
Rodrigo is alive and well!"

The cheerful servants went into
the great hall to spread the news, and
soon the noise from the hall was as
great as when a battle had been won.

Cristina sweated beside the fire,
looking for firewood that might fit
inside Lord Rodrigo's armour and
keep him straight. Then she slipped
round to the stables to steal hay
from the horses.

Babieca was eating quietly and he turned his white head towards her. Cristina had always been afraid of horses. She reached out a hand and stroked the great charger on the nose. It was softer than any silk she had ever felt. Babieca snorted softly. Cristina managed to smile and let out a long breath. "You like me, then? That will help."

She took the scarecrow stuffing back to the bedroom. The guard gave her a curious look, but Lady Jimena came to the door and told him the girl could come and go freely.

The doctor had cleaned the arrow wound on El Cid's neck and the blood had stopped flowing. Cristina knew that only happened when an animal died. Lady Jimena dressed him in a clean, white shirt and then she helped the doctor strap the knight's armour back in place.

By the time they'd finished, the palace was quiet. The knights had gone off to their beds, to be ready for battle the next day. Lady Jimena told the guard outside the door to get himself some supper in the kitchens.

When the corridors were empty,
the three struggled to carry the
corpse down to the stables. Lady
Jimena was strong, and Cristina
found new strength to help her.

Babieca the warhorse was wary
of the scent of the dead man. As the
doctor and the lady struggled to

push El Cid over the saddle, Cristina spoke quietly to the horse and stroked his nose.

They found straps to bind the warrior's legs to the stirrups, and the wooden frame under the armour was tied to the back of the saddle.

Anyone close by could see how El Cid was held there. But the Berbers would not be that close.

Lady Jimena climbed onto the side of the stall with El Cid's helmet and slid it into place. Finally, they dressed the girl in a squire's tunic and placed a wide, leather hat on her head to hide her face.

The scarecrow knight was ready, and the cockerel crowed to tell them dawn was breaking.

Lady Jimena was as dusty as the stable floor and hurried off to change while the doctor sank into the straw, exhausted.

Sleepy grooms and squires began to enter the stables. When they saw Cristina holding Babieca, they woke up and began to race to get their own knights' horses ready.

Lady Jimena was soon changed into a fine, silk dress and came back to give orders to the knights. She stood at the head of Babieca and called to the men in armour.

"My lord Rodrigo has hurt his throat with the scratch from that arrow. He has lost his voice. But he has written what he wants you to do."

She read from a sheet of paper: "Ride out and form a line facing our Berber enemies. The foot soldiers will form lines behind you. The Berbers will think El Cid is dead and they will become careless. When you are all lined up and ready, then my lord will ride out and stand on the hilltop behind you."

The knights nodded and began their march through the dust-choked streets of the city. They reached the gates and followed the orders of Lady Jimena. The Berber army had risen with the sun and they were in a happy mood.

Inside the city gates, Lady Jimena whispered to Cristina. "Scared?"

"Yes," Cristina said.

"Not as scared as the Berbers will be when they see El Cid ride out!" the lady said.

Cristina laughed and her fear melted. She led Babieca out on to the hilltop. Babieca, the idiot, led by Cristina ... the *babieca*.

From her place above the battlefield, the coward-girl saw it all. The Berber army seemed to take a step backwards when she appeared. By the time the knights of Castile charged, they were almost running away.

The defeat of the Berbers that day is there in the history books ... and so is the tale of El Cid's last battle – the knight of sticks and straw.

The girl turned to the horse. "I'll never be scared of scarecrows again," she said.

You never know how brave you are until you are tested.

Cristina the *babieca* had passed the test.

Epilogue

Rodrigo Díaz de Vivar, known as
El Cid, was born around the year
1040, so he was almost 60 years
old when he died in battle with
the Berbers. He lived in Castile
in Spain and his country was for
ever under attack from armies
from North Africa – enemies
like the Berbers.

Rodrigo trained as a knight,
and was so good the king made
him Chief General of the Castile
army. In one battle against
Aragon, Rodrigo faced a mighty
enemy knight. The two men

fought hand to hand while their armies looked on. Rodrigo won, and from then on he was known as El Cid – The Champion.

El Cid was a great war leader because he found new ways to defeat the enemies of Castile. He would surprise enemy armies by doing something they didn't expect. He also liked to frighten his enemies – he thought a scared enemy was a beaten enemy, even before the battle started.

In 1074 (aged 34), Rodrigo married Jimena of Oviedo. (She may have been the daughter of El Cid's greatest enemy.) She was said to be one of the most beautiful women in the world.

For about seven years, Rodrigo was sent away from Castile because he upset King Alfonso. He often upset great lords! But when Castile was under attack, the king begged El Cid to come home. Rodrigo became so powerful he was almost a king in his own land.

Then, in 1099, the Berbers attacked Valencia. Rodrigo rode out to attack Berber food and treasure stores, but was hit by an arrow and died.

It is said that Queen Jimena had the idea of tying his corpse to the horse so he could ride out one last time. The Berbers had thought he was dead ... and they were right! When El Cid appeared, they were so terrified they ran away, back to their boats.

The story of his horse – Babieca the stupid – is supposed to be true. The horse lived to the age of 40, but after his master died no one ever rode him again. Babieca died two years after El Cid.

TERRY DEARY'S TALES